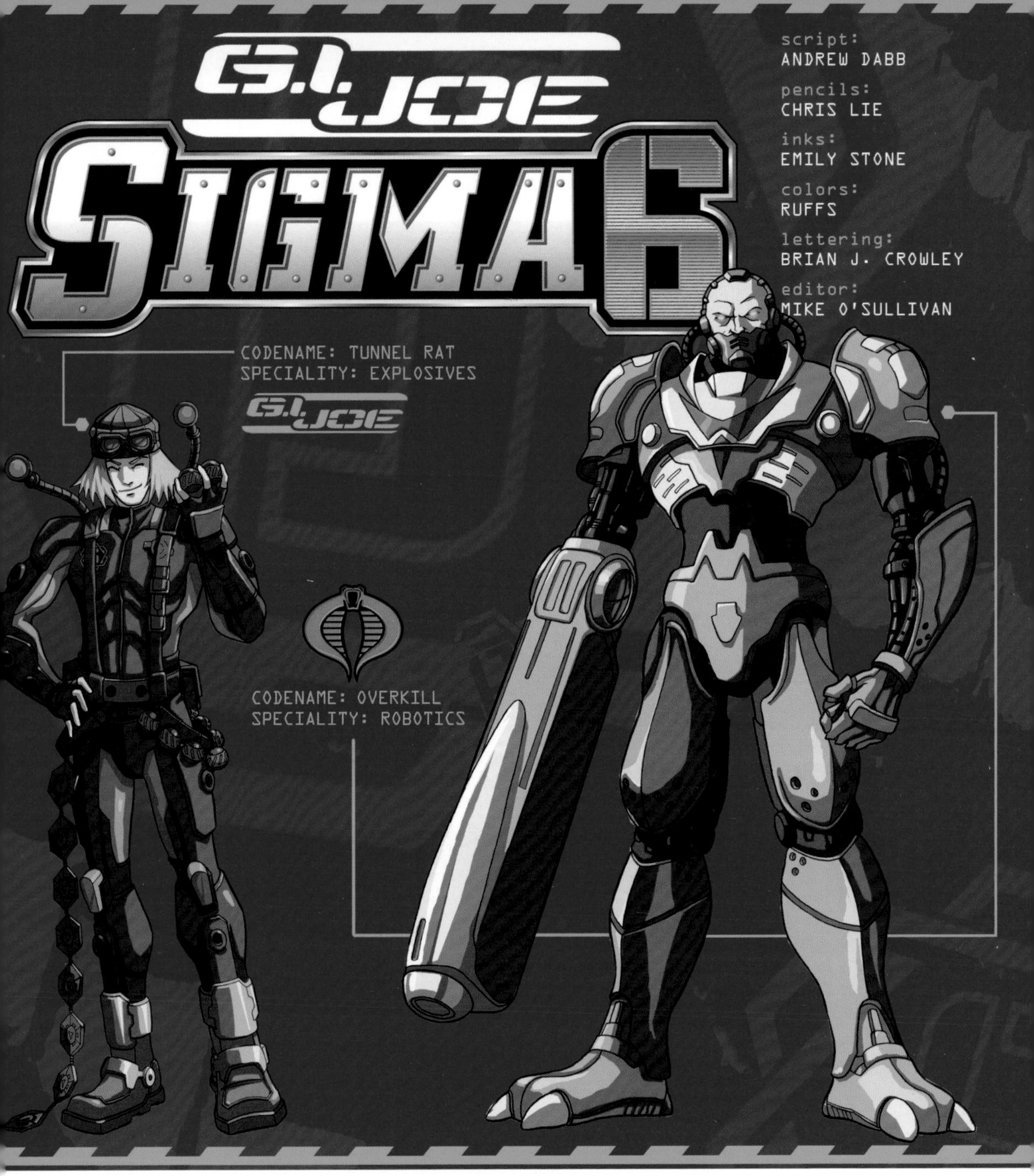
G.I. JOE
SIGMA 6
script:
ANDREW DABB
pencils:
CHRIS LIE
inks:
EMILY STONE
colors:
RUFFS
lettering:
BRIAN J. CROWLEY
editor:
MIKE O'SULLIVAN
CODENAME: TUNNEL RAT
SPECIALITY: EXPLOSIVES
G.I. JOE
CODENAME: OVERKILL
SPECIALITY: ROBOTICS

WIDGETS

visit us at www.abdopublishing.com

Exclusive reinforced library bound edition published in 2008 by Spotlight, a division of ABDO Publishing Group, Edina, Minnesota. This edition is produced under agreement with Devils Due Publishing, Inc. www.devilsdue.net

Library of Congress Cataloging-in-Publication Data

Dabb, Andrew.
  Widgets / script, Andrew Dabb ; pencils, Chris Lie ; inks, Emily Stone ; colors, Ruffs ; lettering, Brian J. Crowley ; editor, Mike O'Sullivan. -- Exclusive reinforced library bound ed.
      p. cm. -- (G.I. Joe SIGMA 6)
    Revision of issue 3 (Feb. 2006) of G.I. Joe Sigma 6.
    ISBN-13: 978-1-59961-374-1
    ISBN-10: 1-59961-374-3
      1. Graphic novels. I. Lie, Chris. II. O'Sullivan, Mike. III. G.I. Joe SIGMA 6. 3. IV. Title.

PN6727.D23W53 2008
741.5'973--dc22
                                                                    2006052228

All Spotlight books have reinforced library bindings
and are manufactured in the United States of America.

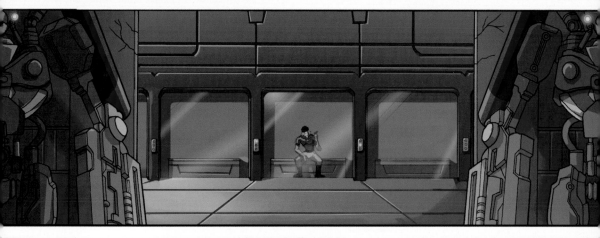

ALONE.

CAPTURED.

WITHOUT MY SIGMA SUIT.

THIS IS THE *BEST DAY* OF MY LIFE!

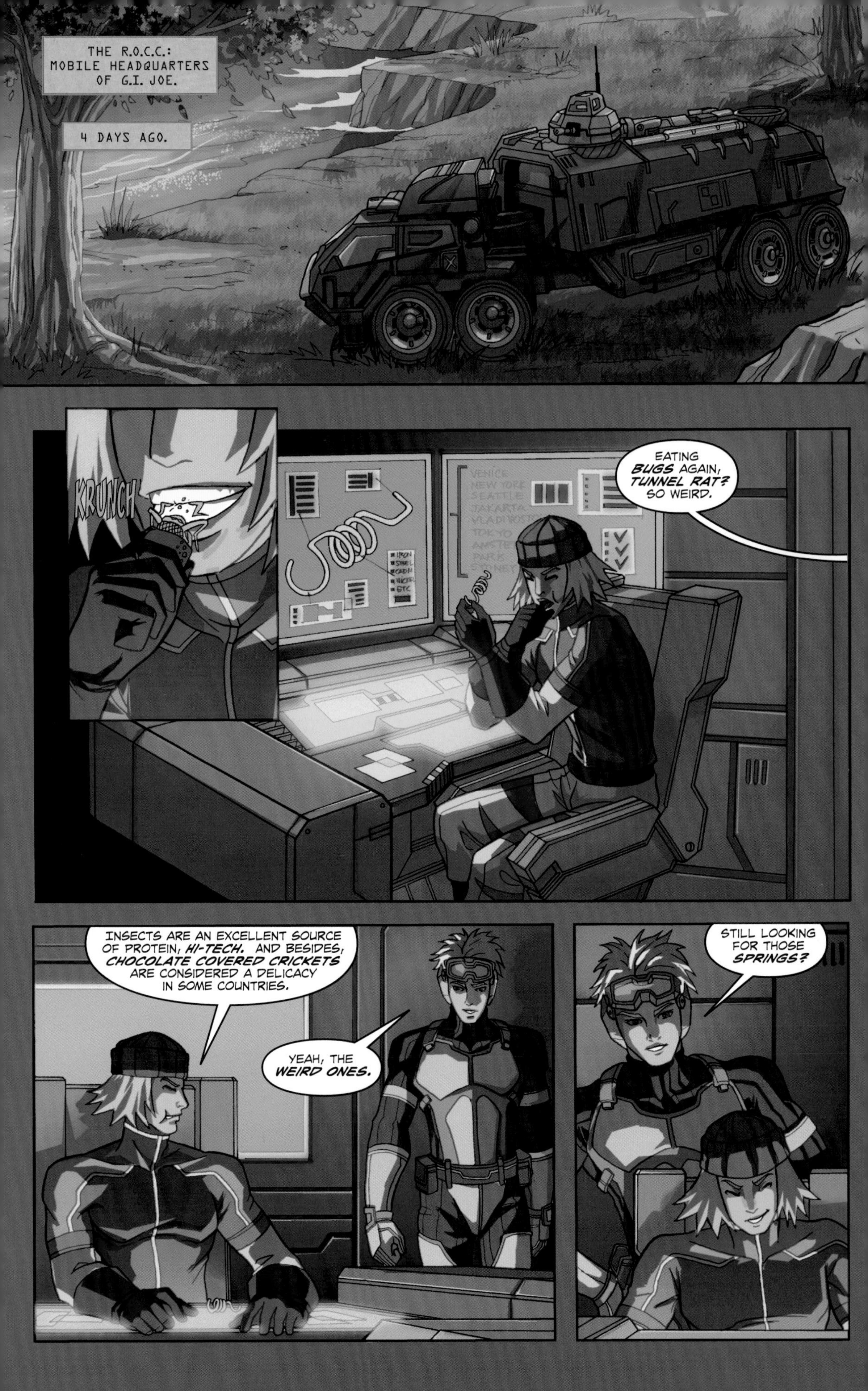
THE R.O.C.C.: MOBILE HEADQUARTERS OF G.I. JOE.
4 DAYS AGO.
KRUNCH
EATING BUGS AGAIN, TUNNEL RAT? SO WEIRD.
INSECTS ARE AN EXCELLENT SOURCE OF PROTEIN, HI-TECH. AND BESIDES, CHOCOLATE COVERED CRICKETS ARE CONSIDERED A DELICACY IN SOME COUNTRIES.
YEAH, THE WEIRD ONES.
STILL LOOKING FOR THOSE SPRINGS?

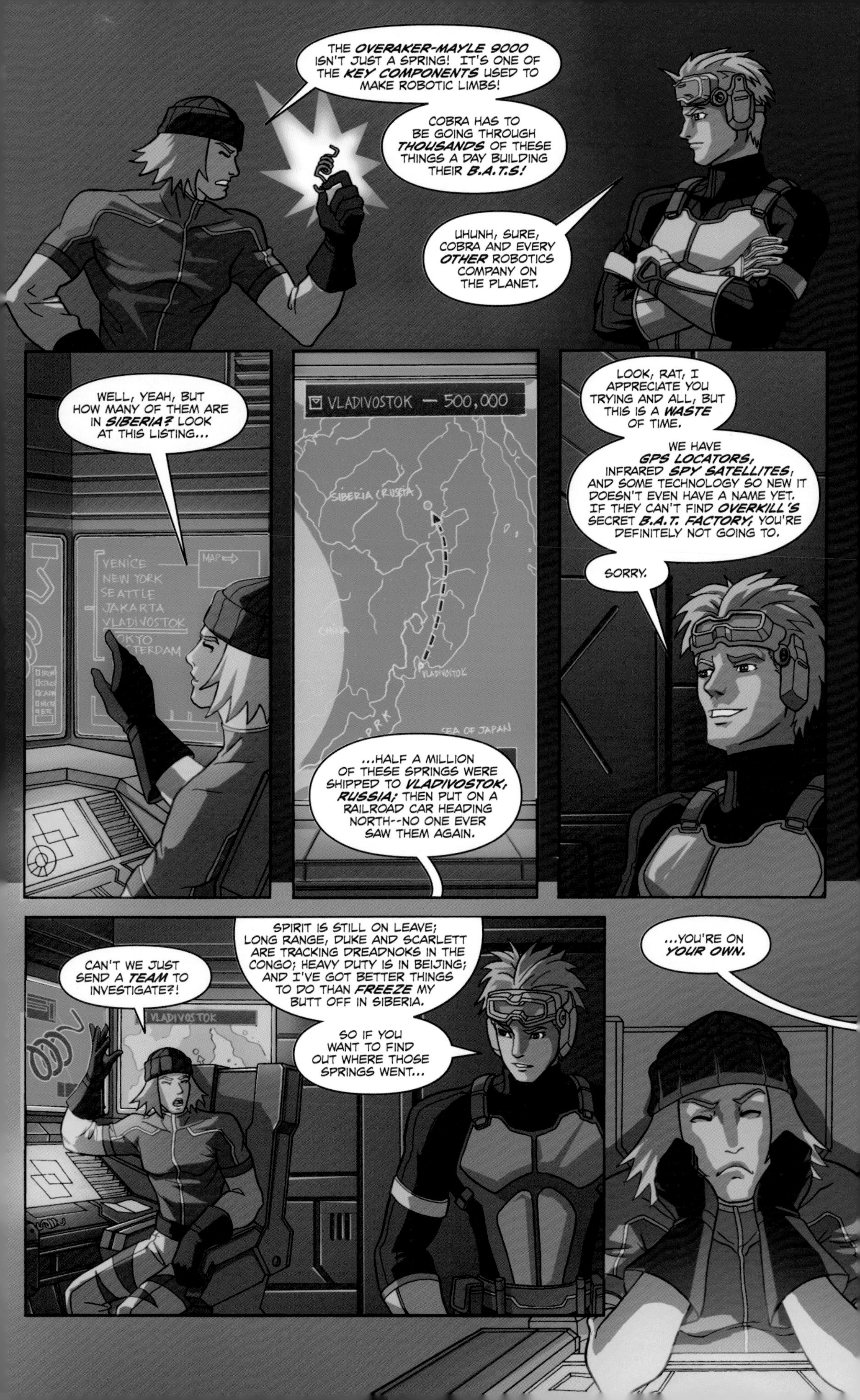
THE OVERAKER-MAYLE 9000 ISN'T JUST A SPRING! IT'S ONE OF THE KEY COMPONENTS USED TO MAKE ROBOTIC LIMBS!
COBRA HAS TO BE GOING THROUGH THOUSANDS OF THESE THINGS A DAY BUILDING THEIR B.A.T.S!
UHUNH, SURE, COBRA AND EVERY OTHER ROBOTICS COMPANY ON THE PLANET.
WELL, YEAH, BUT HOW MANY OF THEM ARE IN SIBERIA? LOOK AT THIS LISTING...
VENICE
NEW YORK
SEATTLE
JAKARTA
VLADIVOSTOK
MAP
VLADIVOSTOK — 500,000
SIBERIA (RUSSIA)
CHINA
VLADIVOSTOK
SEA OF JAPAN
...HALF A MILLION OF THESE SPRINGS WERE SHIPPED TO VLADIVOSTOK, RUSSIA; THEN PUT ON A RAILROAD CAR HEADING NORTH--NO ONE EVER SAW THEM AGAIN.
LOOK, RAT, I APPRECIATE YOU TRYING AND ALL, BUT THIS IS A WASTE OF TIME.
WE HAVE GPS LOCATORS, INFRARED SPY SATELLITES, AND SOME TECHNOLOGY SO NEW IT DOESN'T EVEN HAVE A NAME YET. IF THEY CAN'T FIND OVERKILL'S SECRET B.A.T. FACTORY, YOU'RE DEFINITELY NOT GOING TO.
SORRY.
CAN'T WE JUST SEND A TEAM TO INVESTIGATE?!
VLADIVOSTOK
SPIRIT IS STILL ON LEAVE; LONG RANGE, DUKE AND SCARLETT ARE TRACKING DREADNOKS IN THE CONGO; HEAVY DUTY IS IN BEIJING; AND I'VE GOT BETTER THINGS TO DO THAN FREEZE MY BUTT OFF IN SIBERIA.
SO IF YOU WANT TO FIND OUT WHERE THOSE SPRINGS WENT...
...YOU'RE ON YOUR OWN.

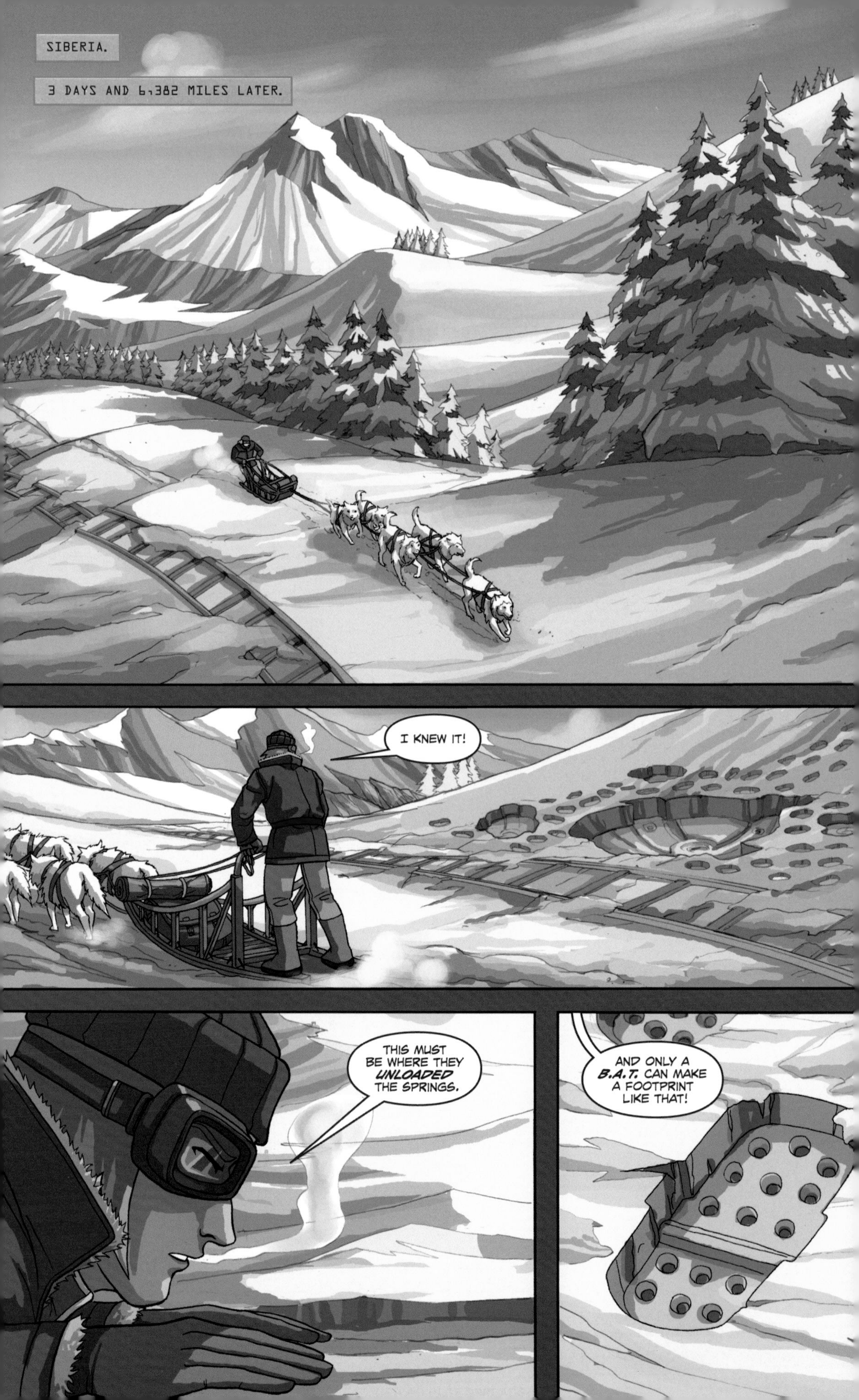
SIBERIA.
3 DAYS AND 6,382 MILES LATER.
I KNEW IT!
THIS MUST BE WHERE THEY *UNLOADED* THE SPRINGS.
AND ONLY A *B.A.T.* CAN MAKE A FOOTPRINT LIKE THAT!

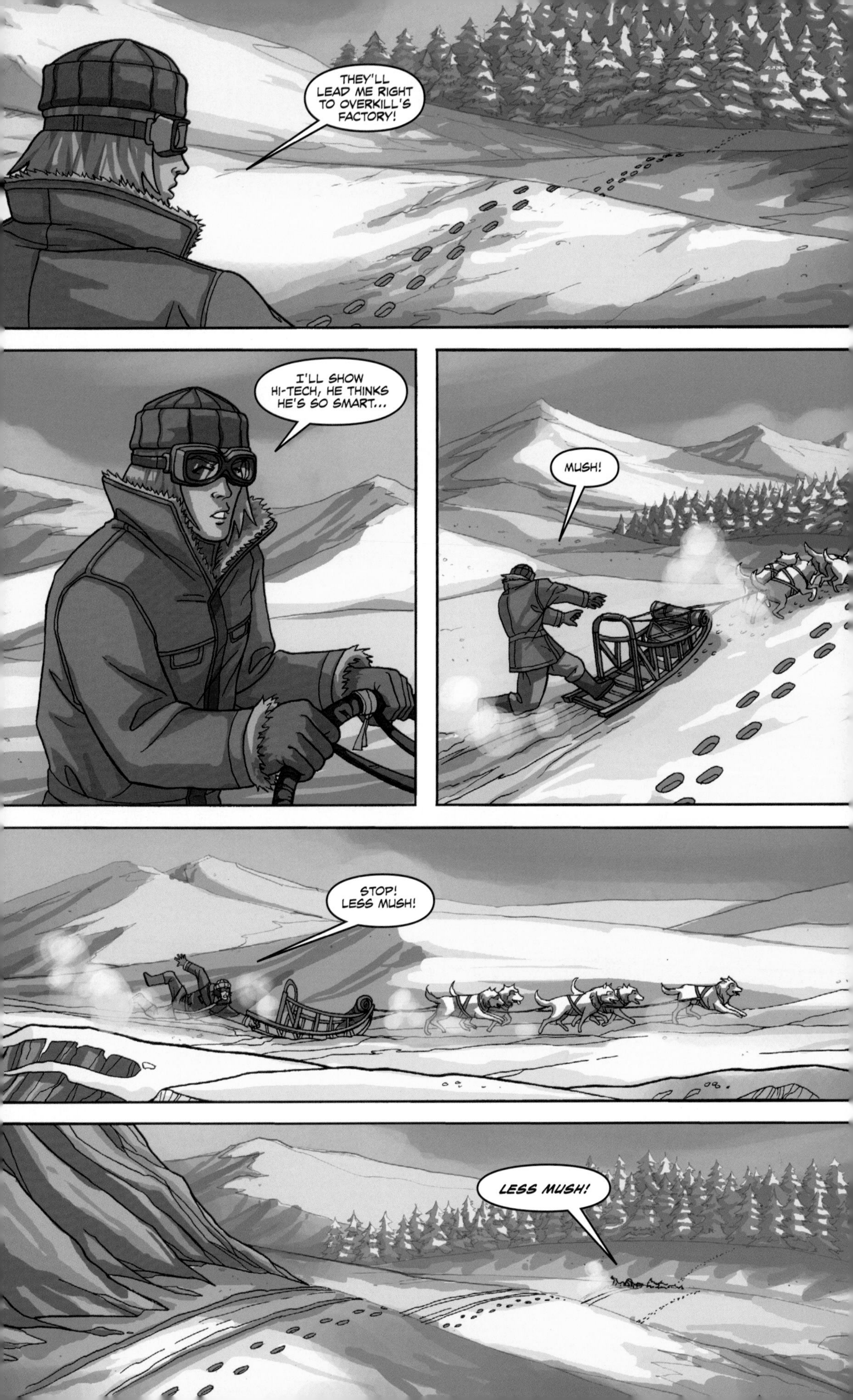
THEY'LL LEAD ME RIGHT TO OVERKILL'S FACTORY!
I'LL SHOW HI-TECH, HE THINKS HE'S SO SMART...
MUSH!
STOP! LESS MUSH!
LESS MUSH!

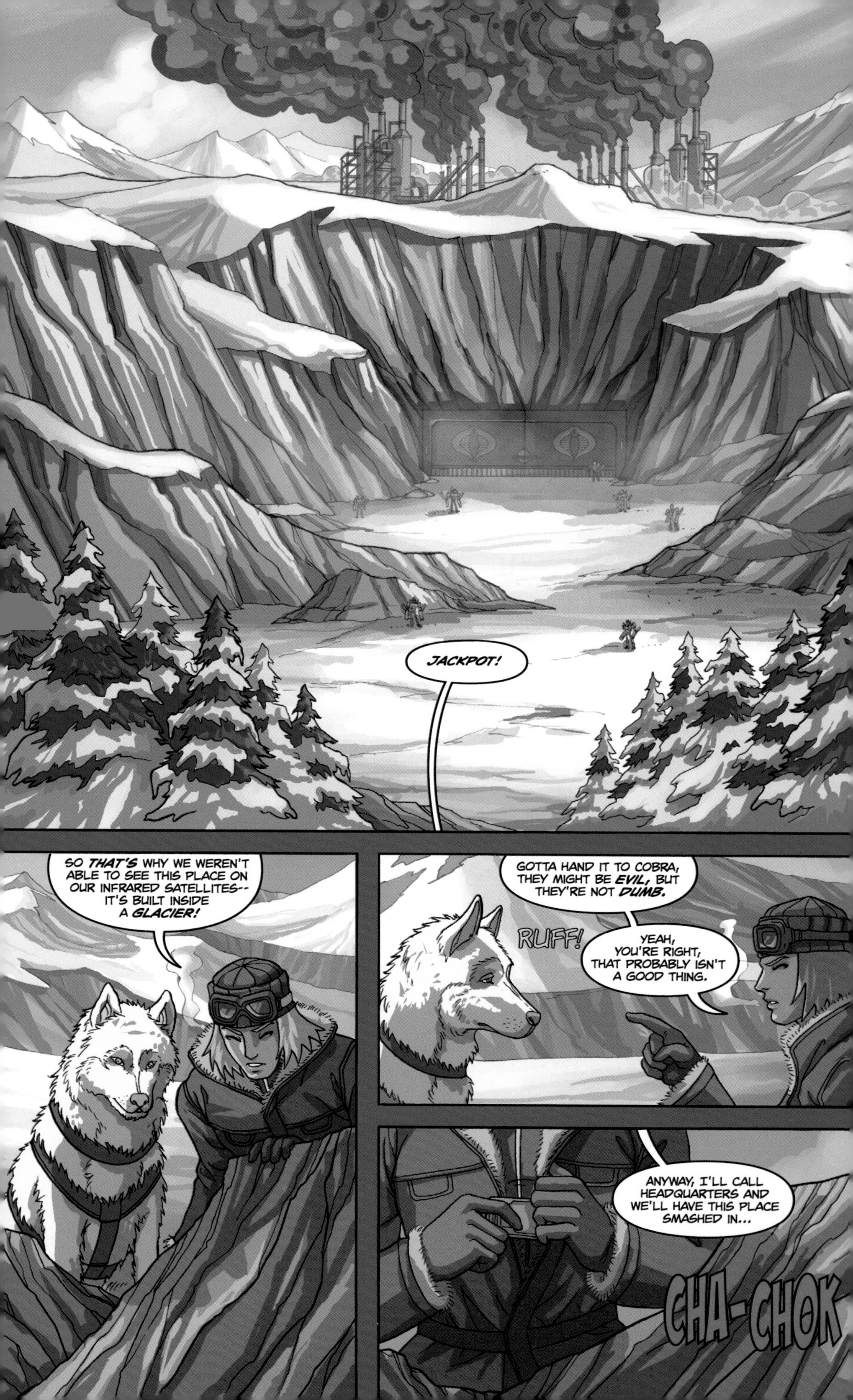
JACKPOT!
SO THAT'S WHY WE WEREN'T ABLE TO SEE THIS PLACE ON OUR INFRARED SATELLITES--IT'S BUILT INSIDE A GLACIER!
GOTTA HAND IT TO COBRA, THEY MIGHT BE EVIL, BUT THEY'RE NOT DUMB.
RUFF!
YEAH, YOU'RE RIGHT, THAT PROBABLY ISN'T A GOOD THING.
ANYWAY, I'LL CALL HEADQUARTERS AND WE'LL HAVE THIS PLACE SMASHED IN...
CHA-CHOK

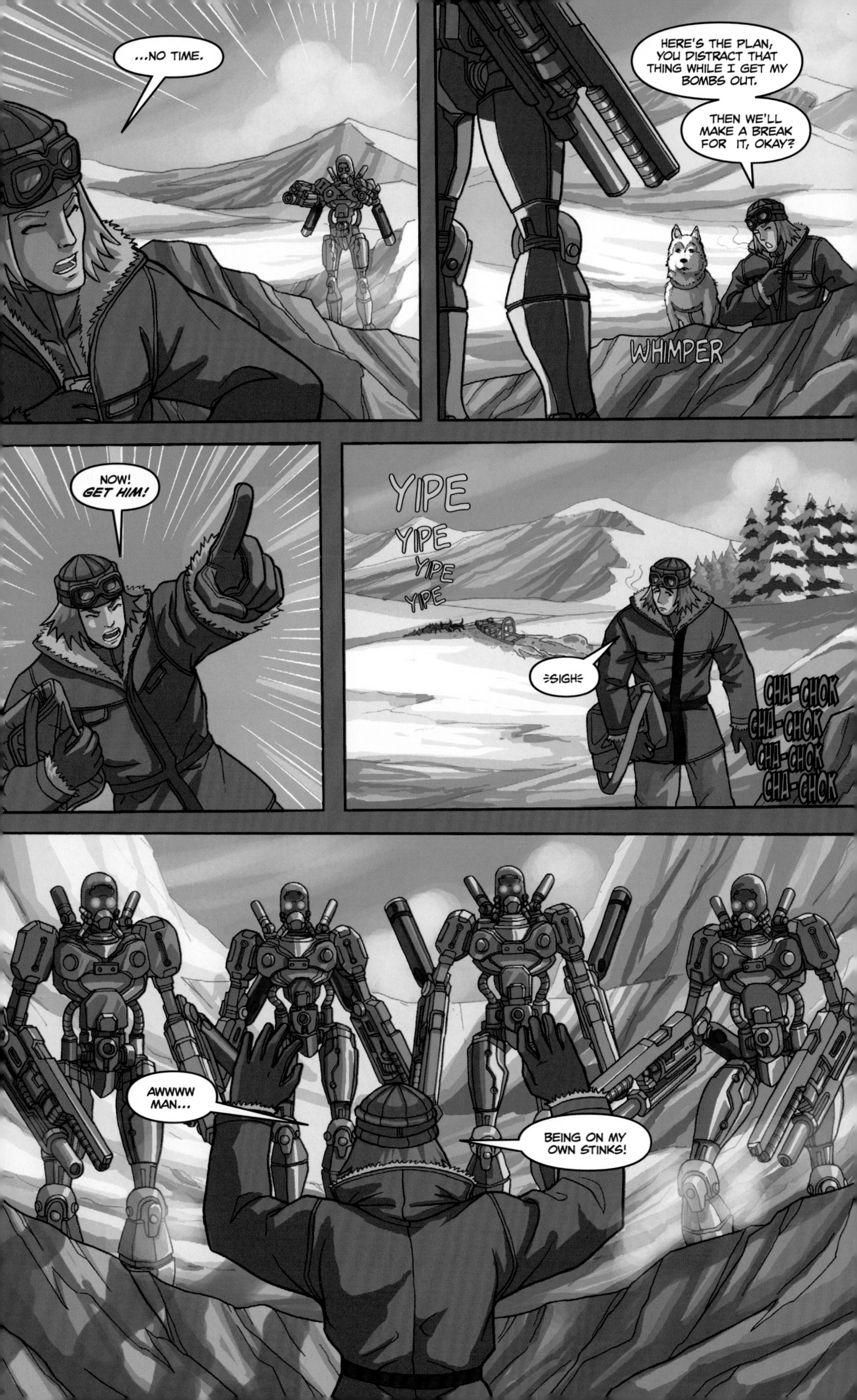
...NO TIME.
HERE'S THE PLAN, YOU DISTRACT THAT THING WHILE I GET MY BOMBS OUT.
THEN WE'LL MAKE A BREAK FOR IT, OKAY?
WHIMPER
NOW! GET HIM!
YIPE
YIPE
YIPE
YIPE
SIGH
CHA-CHOK
CHA-CHOK
CHA-CHOK
CHA-CHOK
AWWWW MAN...
BEING ON MY OWN STINKS!

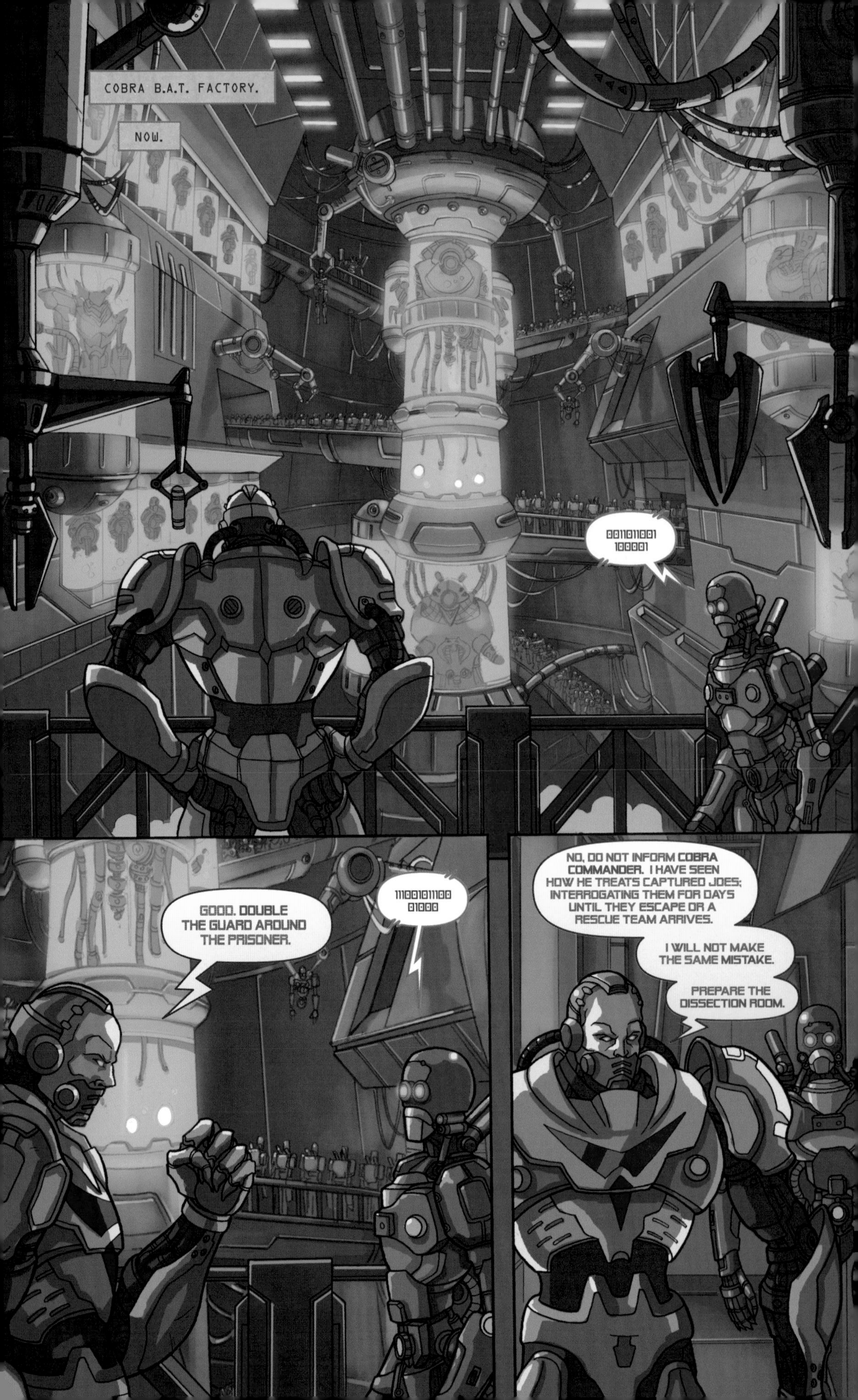
COBRA B.A.T. FACTORY.
NOW.
0011011001 100001
GOOD. DOUBLE THE GUARD AROUND THE PRISONER.
11100101100 01000
NO, DO NOT INFORM COBRA COMMANDER. I HAVE SEEN HOW HE TREATS CAPTURED JOES; INTERROGATING THEM FOR DAYS UNTIL THEY ESCAPE OR A RESCUE TEAM ARRIVES.
I WILL NOT MAKE THE SAME MISTAKE.
PREPARE THE DISSECTION ROOM.

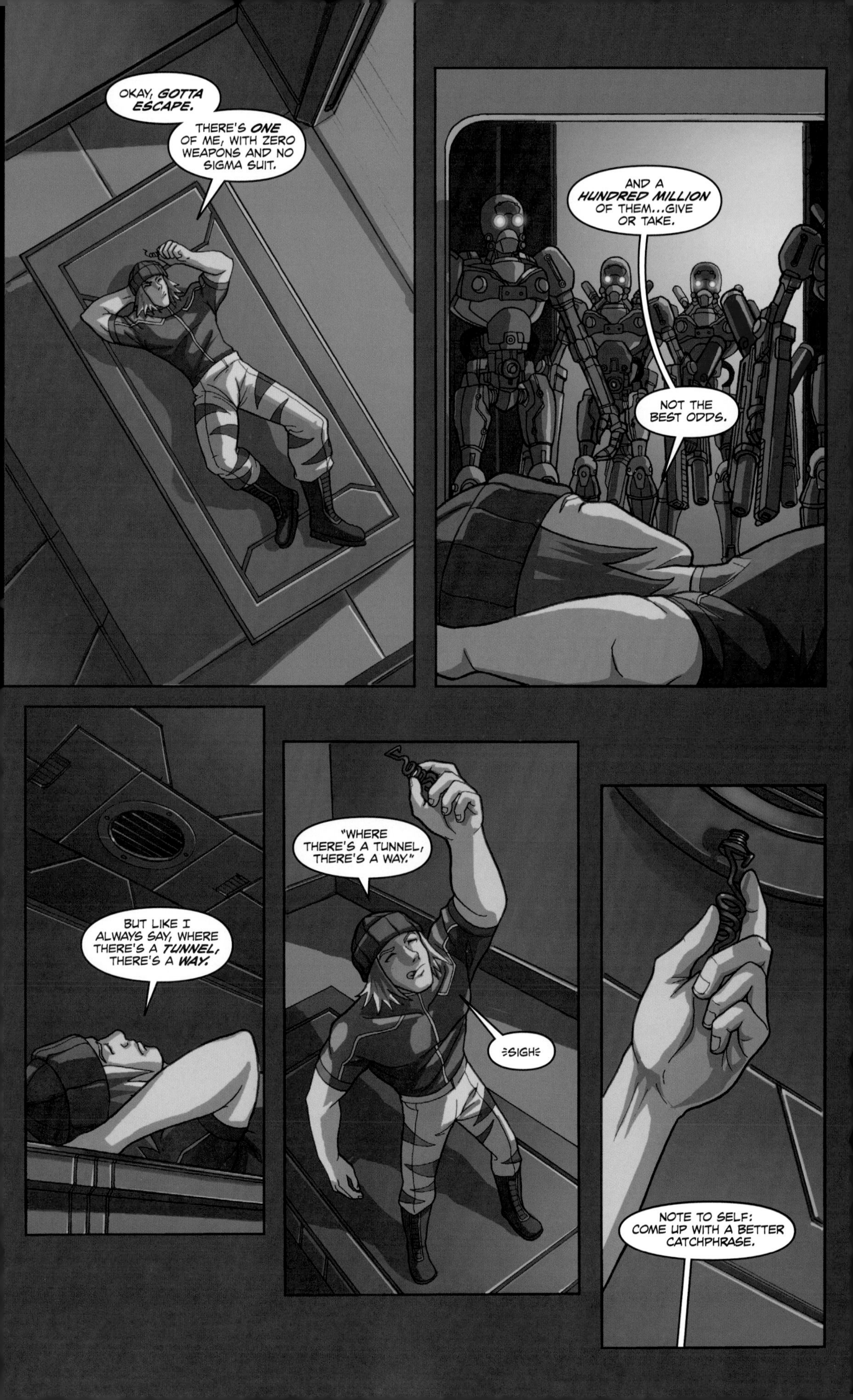
OKAY, GOTTA ESCAPE.
THERE'S ONE OF ME, WITH ZERO WEAPONS AND NO SIGMA SUIT.
AND A HUNDRED MILLION OF THEM...GIVE OR TAKE.
NOT THE BEST ODDS.
BUT LIKE I ALWAYS SAY, WHERE THERE'S A TUNNEL, THERE'S A WAY.
"WHERE THERE'S A TUNNEL, THERE'S A WAY."
=SIGH=
NOTE TO SELF: COME UP WITH A BETTER CATCHPHRASE.

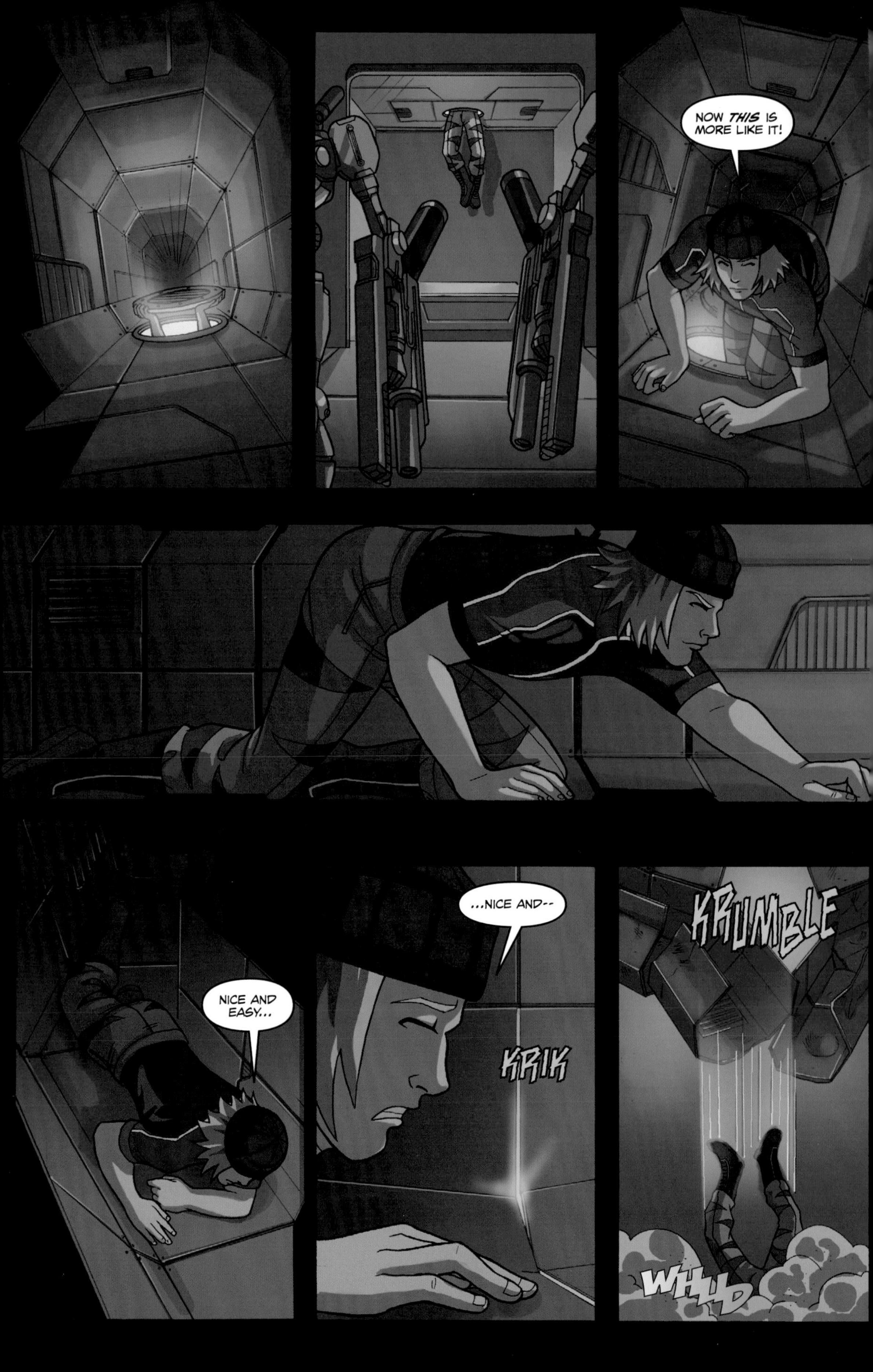
NOW *THIS* IS MORE LIKE IT!
NICE AND EASY...
...NICE AND--
KRIK
KRUMBLE
WHUD

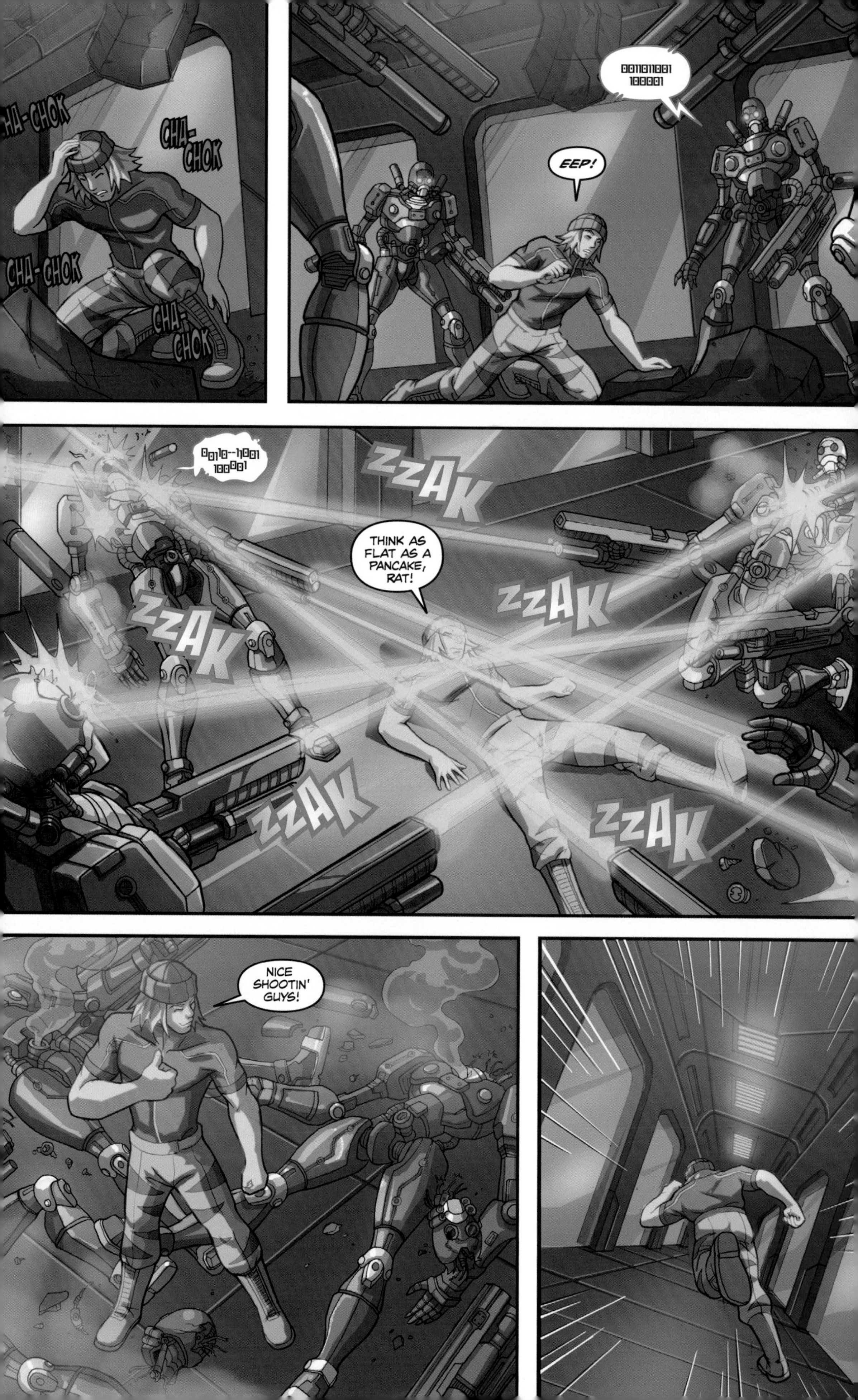

HA-CHOK
CHA-CHOK
CHA-CHOK
CHA-CHOK
0011011001
100001
EEP!
0010--1001
100001
ZZAK
THINK AS FLAT AS A PANCAKE, RAT!
ZZAK
ZZAK
ZZAK
ZZAK
NICE SHOOTIN' GUYS!

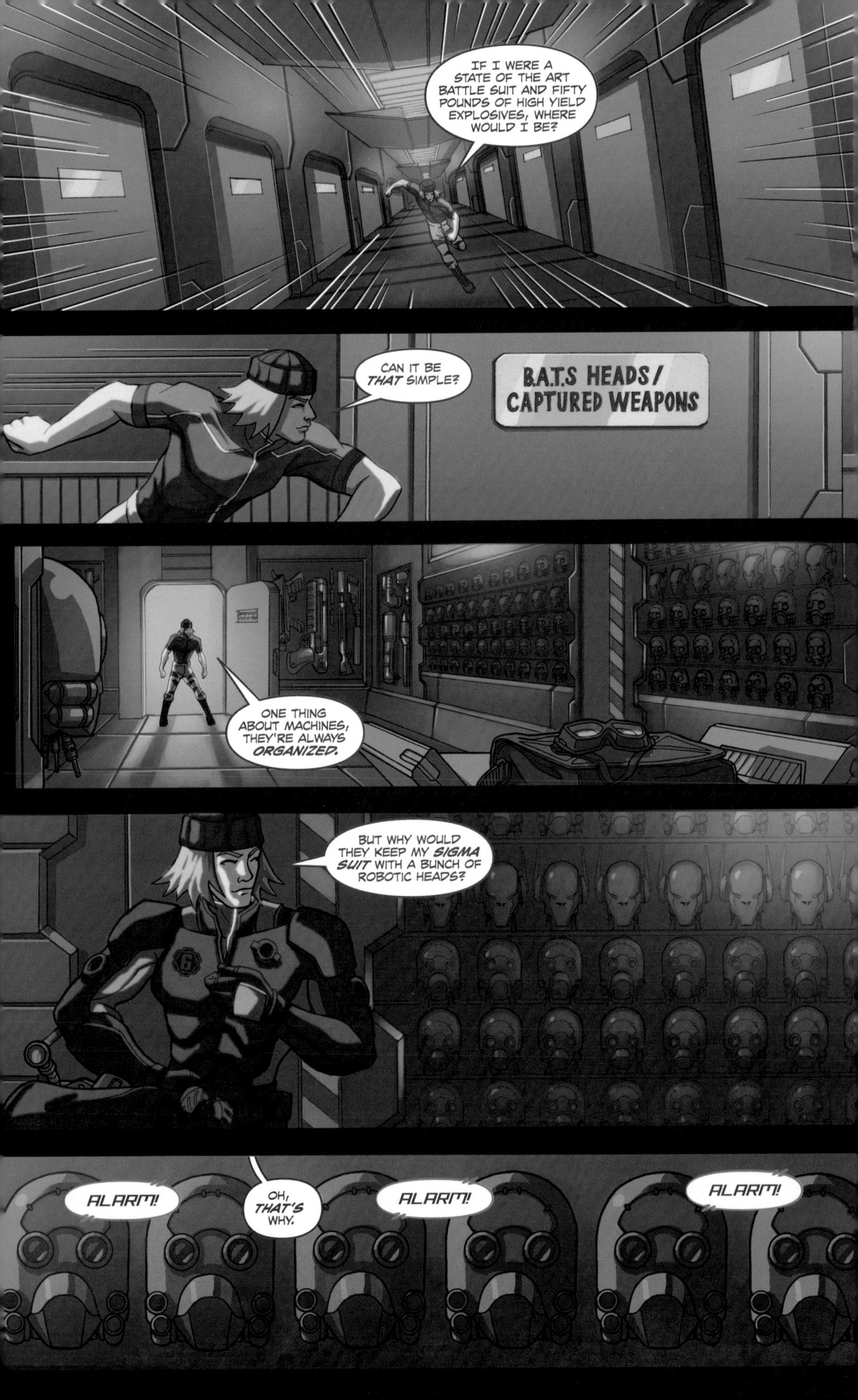
IF I WERE A STATE OF THE ART BATTLE SUIT AND FIFTY POUNDS OF HIGH YIELD EXPLOSIVES, WHERE WOULD I BE?
CAN IT BE THAT SIMPLE?
B.A.T.S HEADS/ CAPTURED WEAPONS
ONE THING ABOUT MACHINES, THEY'RE ALWAYS ORGANIZED.
BUT WHY WOULD THEY KEEP MY SIGMA SUIT WITH A BUNCH OF ROBOTIC HEADS?
ALARM!
OH, THAT'S WHY.
ALARM!
ALARM!

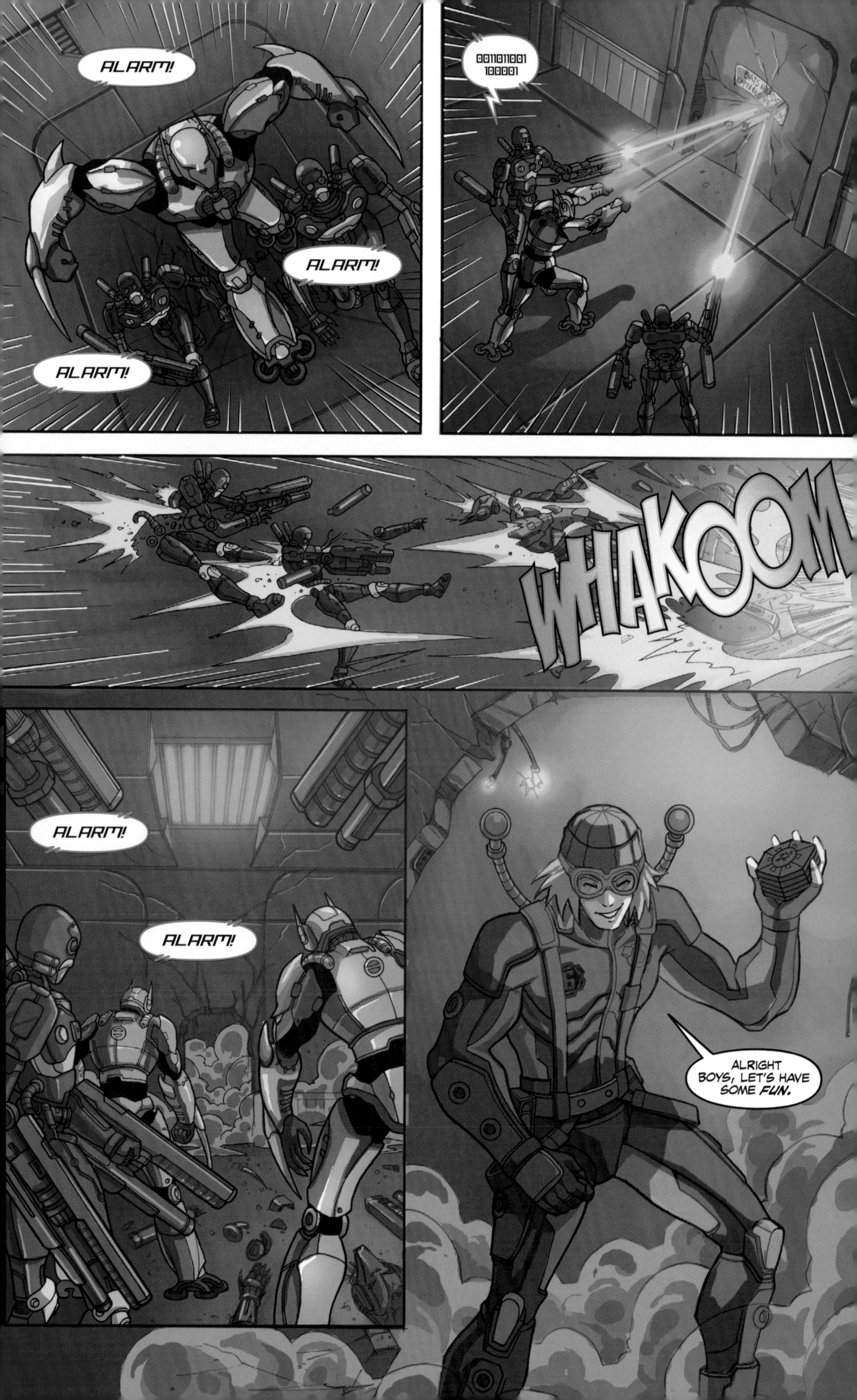
ALARM!
ALARM!
ALARM!
0011011001
100001
WHAKOOM
ALARM!
ALARM!
ALRIGHT BOYS, LET'S HAVE SOME *FUN.*

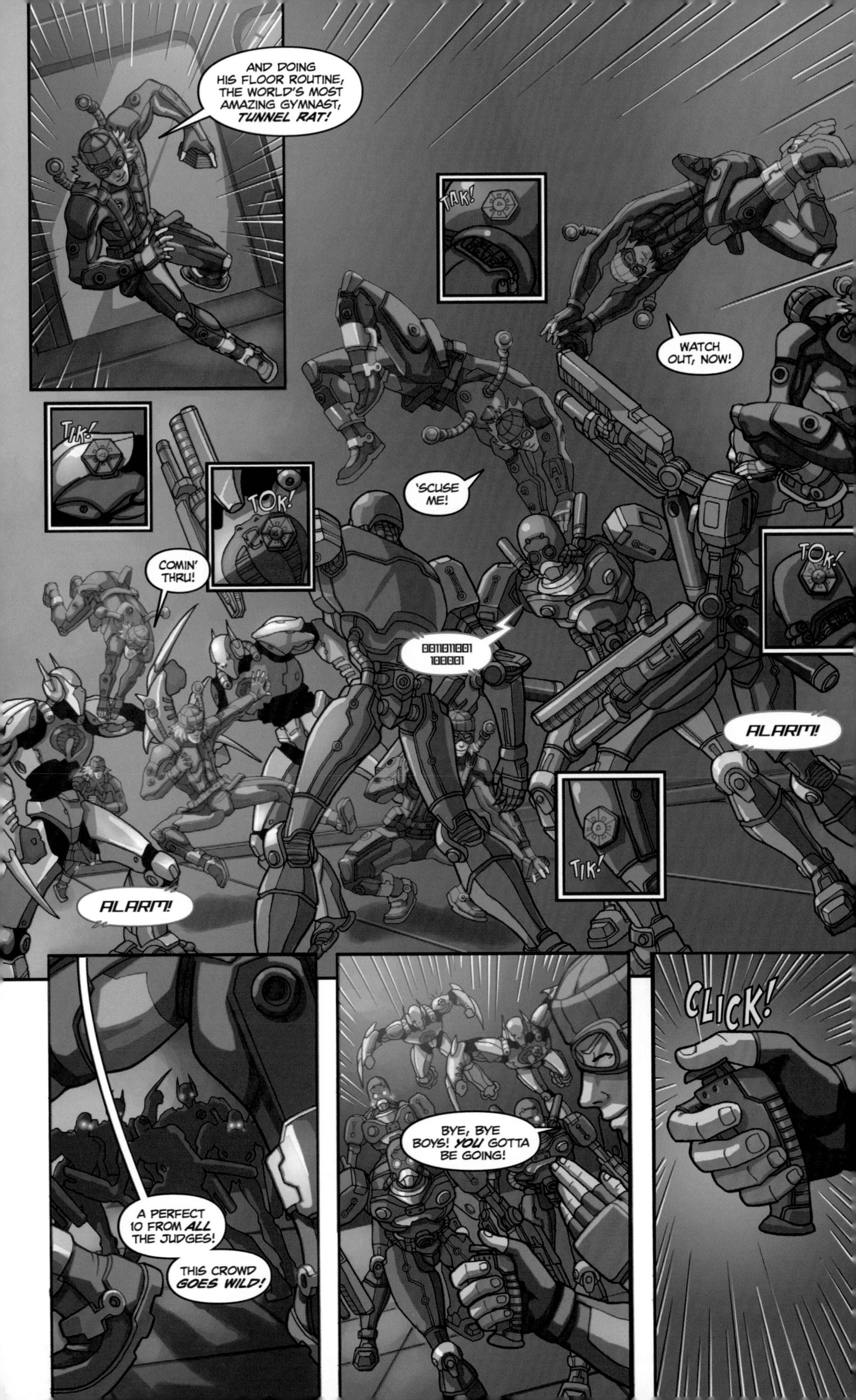
AND DOING HIS FLOOR ROUTINE, THE WORLD'S MOST AMAZING GYMNAST, TUNNEL RAT!
TAK!
WATCH OUT, NOW!
TIK!
TOK!
'SCUSE ME!
COMIN' THRU!
0011011001 100001
TOK!
ALARM!
TIK!
ALARM!
A PERFECT 10 FROM ALL THE JUDGES!
THIS CROWD GOES WILD!
BYE, BYE BOYS! YOU GOTTA BE GOING!
CLICK!

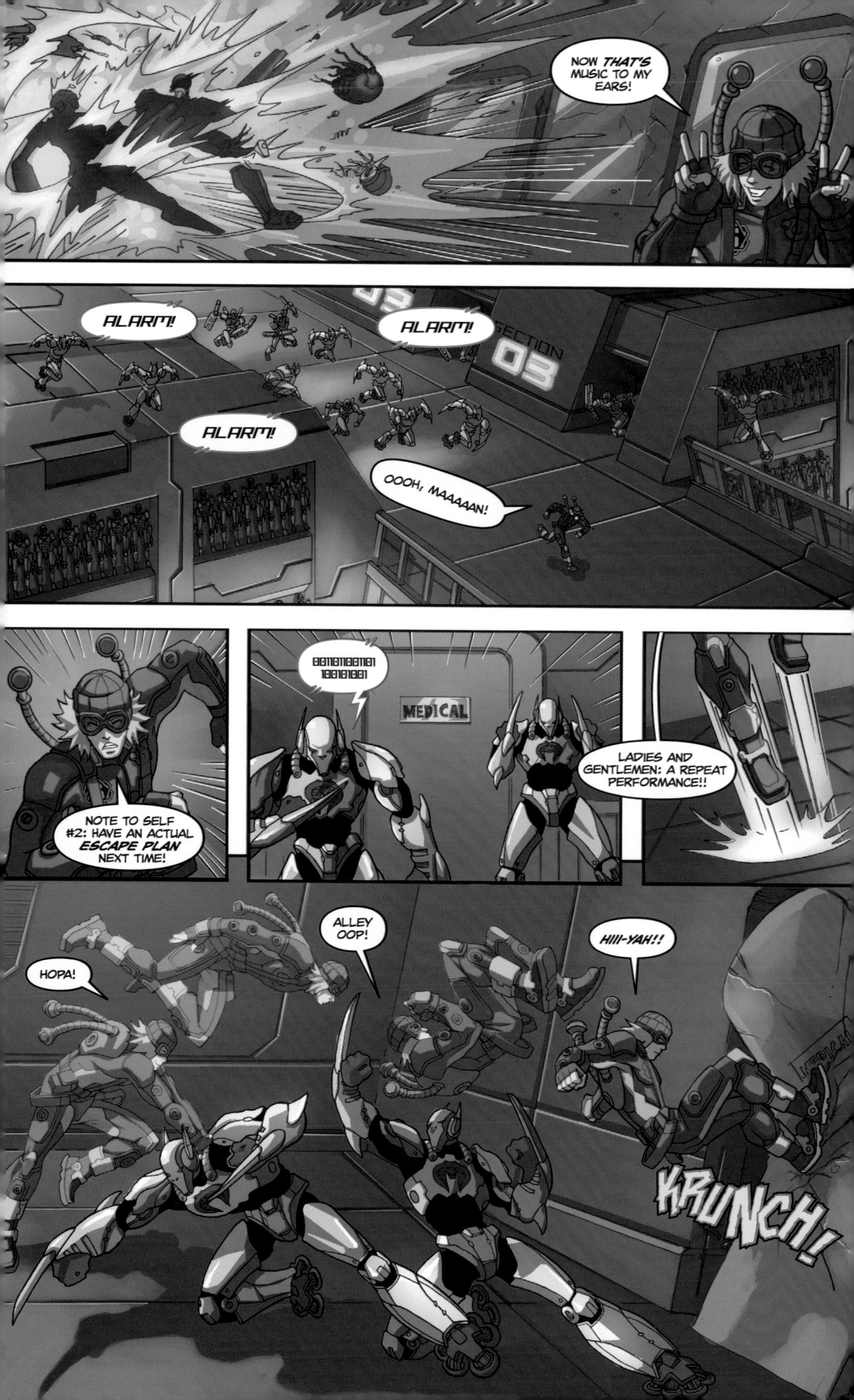
NOW *THAT'S* MUSIC TO MY EARS!
ALARM!
ALARM!
SECTION 03
ALARM!
OOOH, MAAAAAN!
NOTE TO SELF #2: HAVE AN ACTUAL *ESCAPE PLAN* NEXT TIME!
0011011001101 100101001
MEDICAL
LADIES AND GENTLEMEN: A REPEAT PERFORMANCE!!
HOPA!
ALLEY OOP!
HIII-YAH!!
KRUNCH!

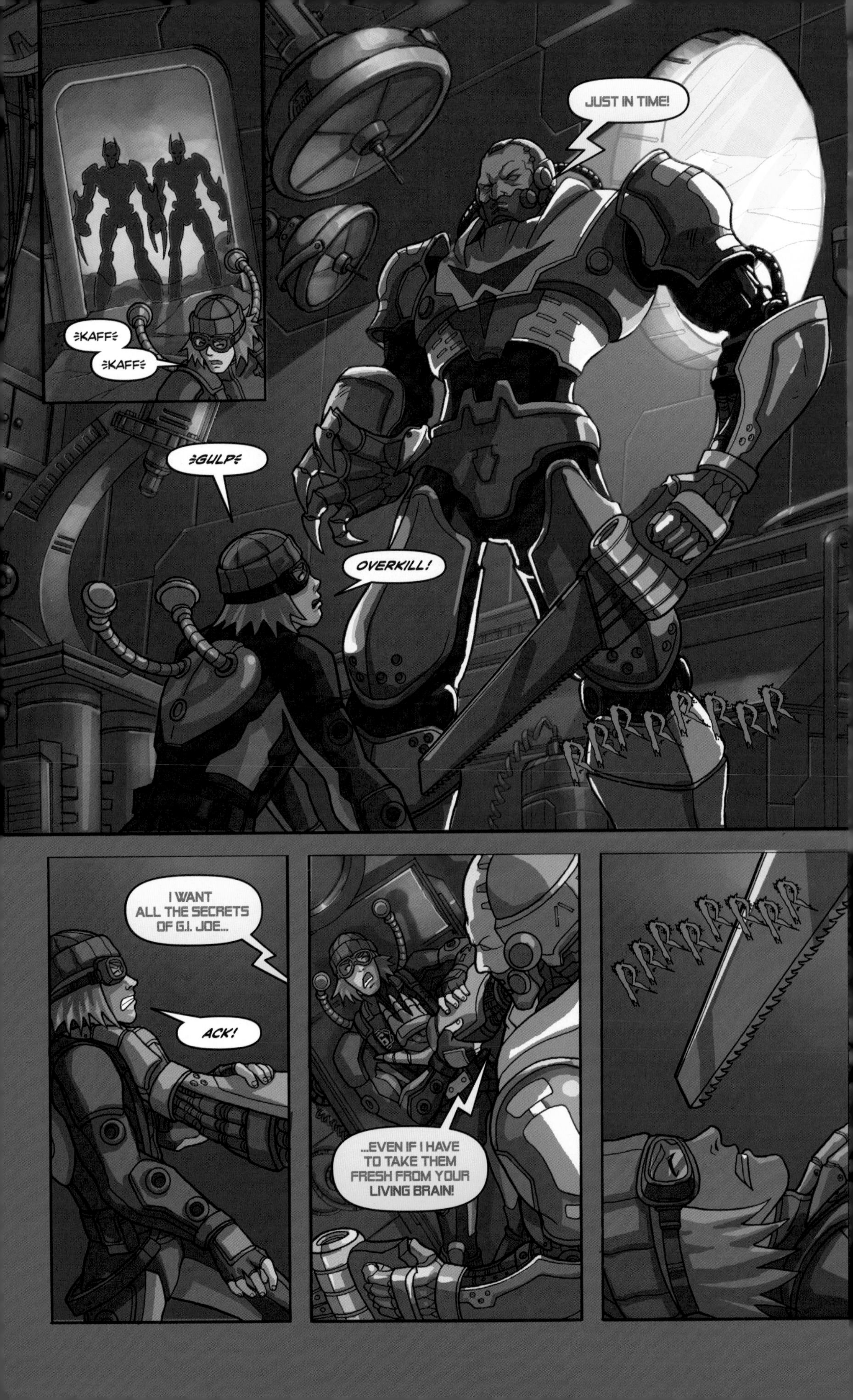

KAFF
KAFF
JUST IN TIME!
GULP
OVERKILL!
RRRRRRRRR
I WANT ALL THE SECRETS OF G.I. JOE...
ACK!
...EVEN IF I HAVE TO TAKE THEM FRESH FROM YOUR LIVING BRAIN!
RRRRRRRRR

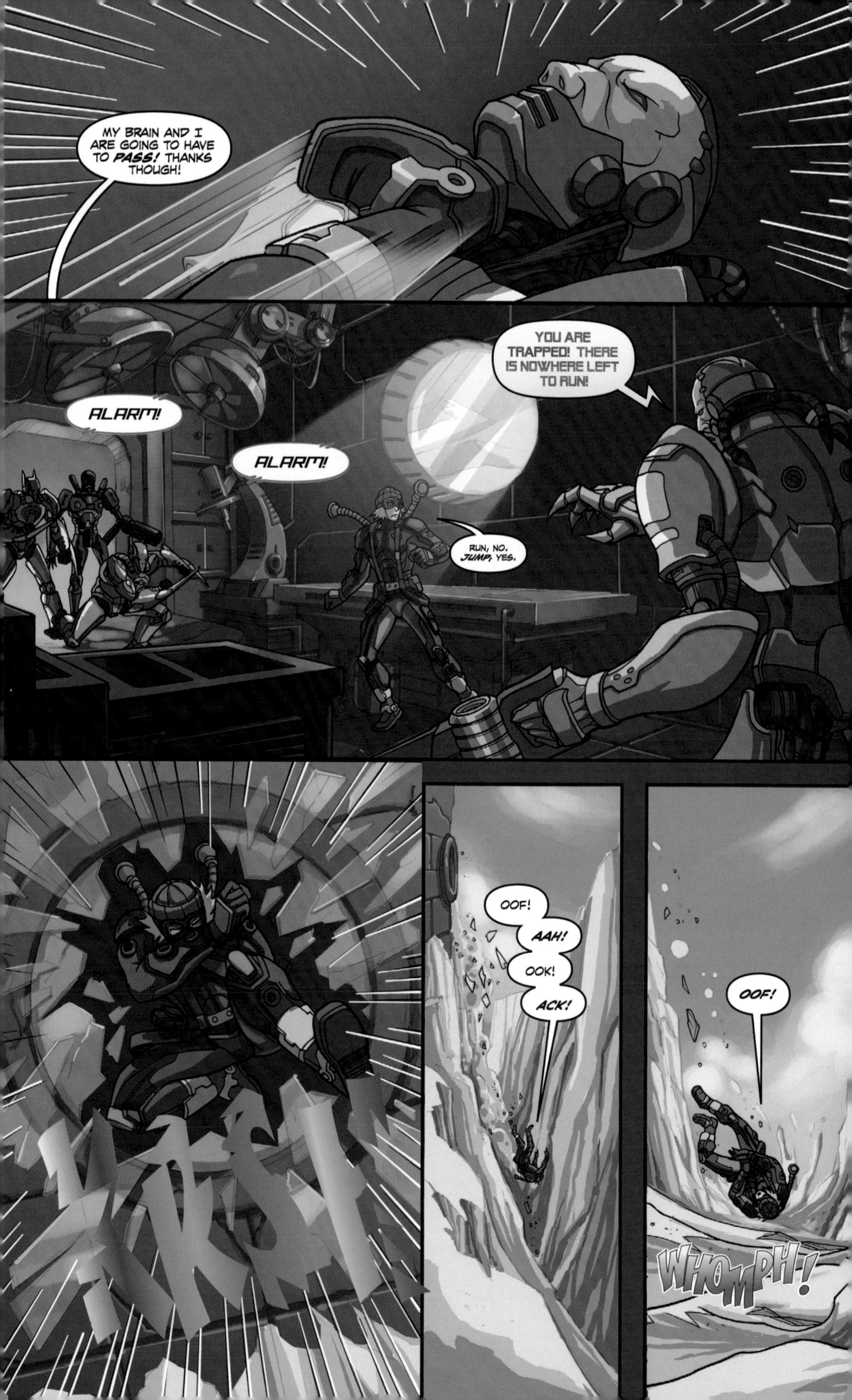
MY BRAIN AND I ARE GOING TO HAVE TO *PASS!* THANKS THOUGH!
YOU ARE TRAPPED! THERE IS NOWHERE LEFT TO RUN!
ALARM!
ALARM!
RUN, NO. *JUMP,* YES.
OOF!
AAH!
OOK!
ACK!
OOF!
WHOMPH!

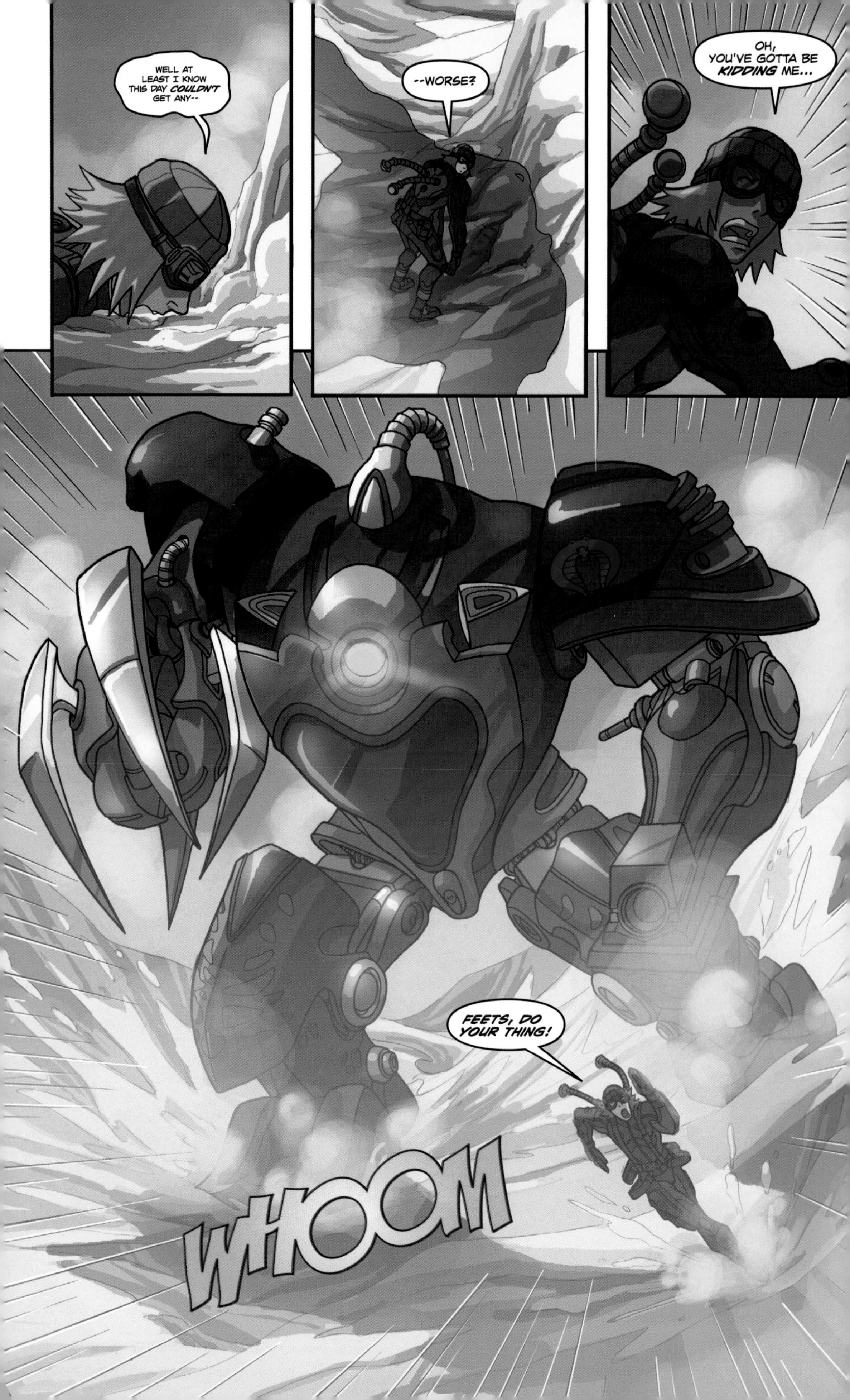
WELL AT LEAST I KNOW THIS DAY COULDN'T GET ANY--
--WORSE?
OH, YOU'VE GOTTA BE KIDDING ME...
FEETS, DO YOUR THING!
WHOOM

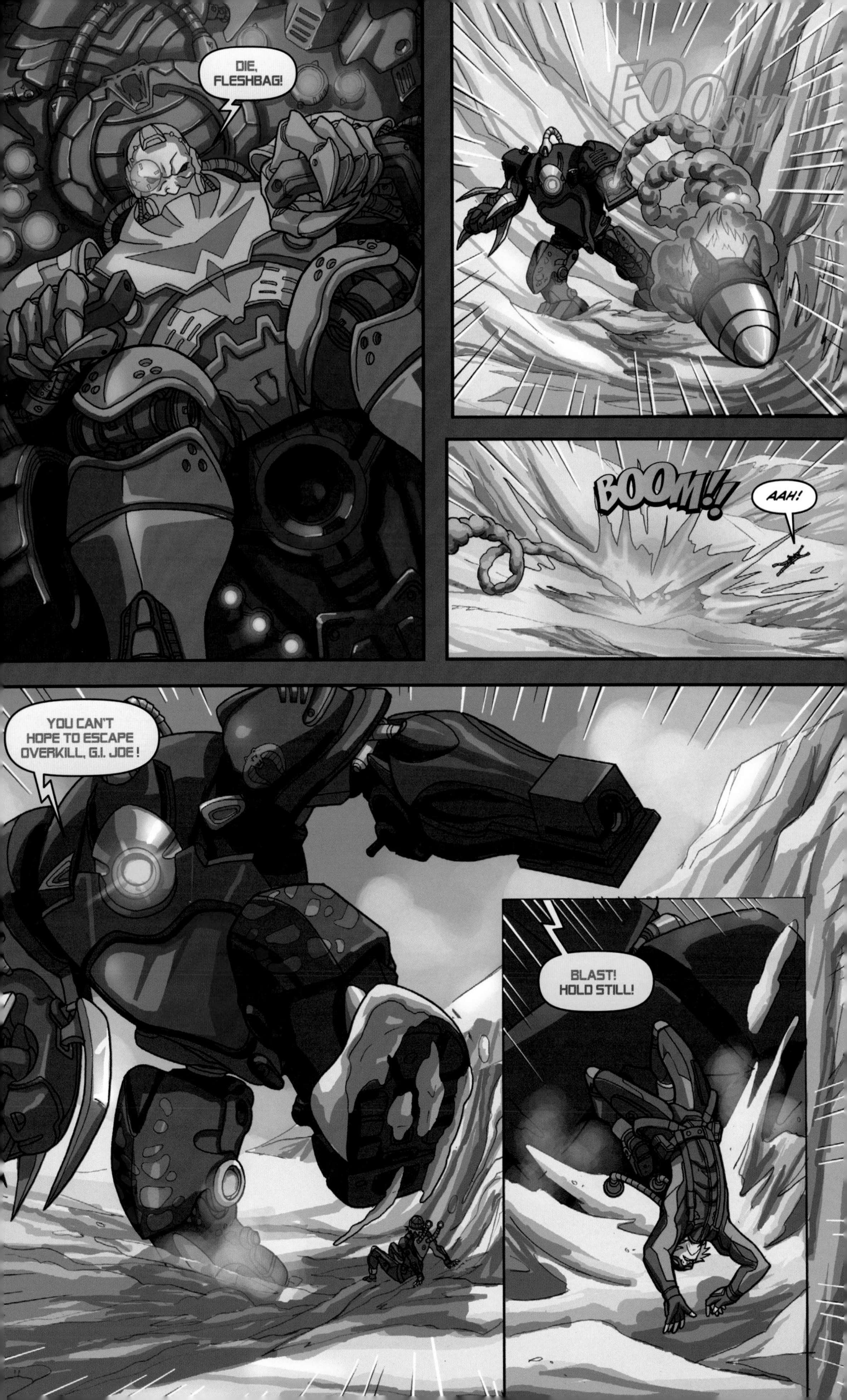
DIE, FLESHBAG!
FOOSH
BOOM!!
AAH!
YOU CAN'T HOPE TO ESCAPE OVERKILL, G.I. JOE!
BLAST! HOLD STILL!

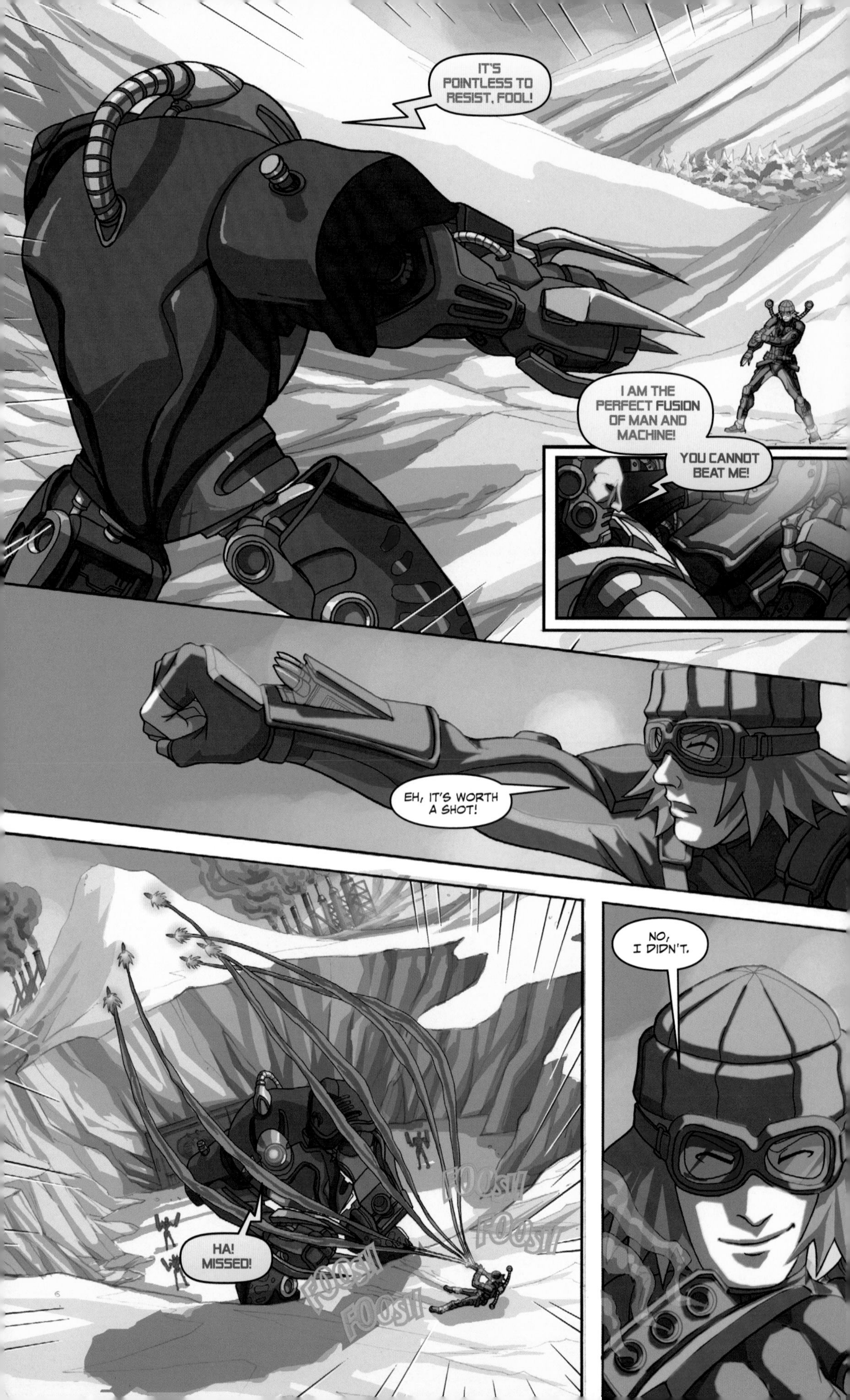
IT'S POINTLESS TO RESIST, FOOL!
I AM THE PERFECT FUSION OF MAN AND MACHINE!
YOU CANNOT BEAT ME!
EH, IT'S WORTH A SHOT!
FOOSH!
FOOSH!
HA! MISSED!
FOOSH!
FOOSH!
NO, I DIDN'T.

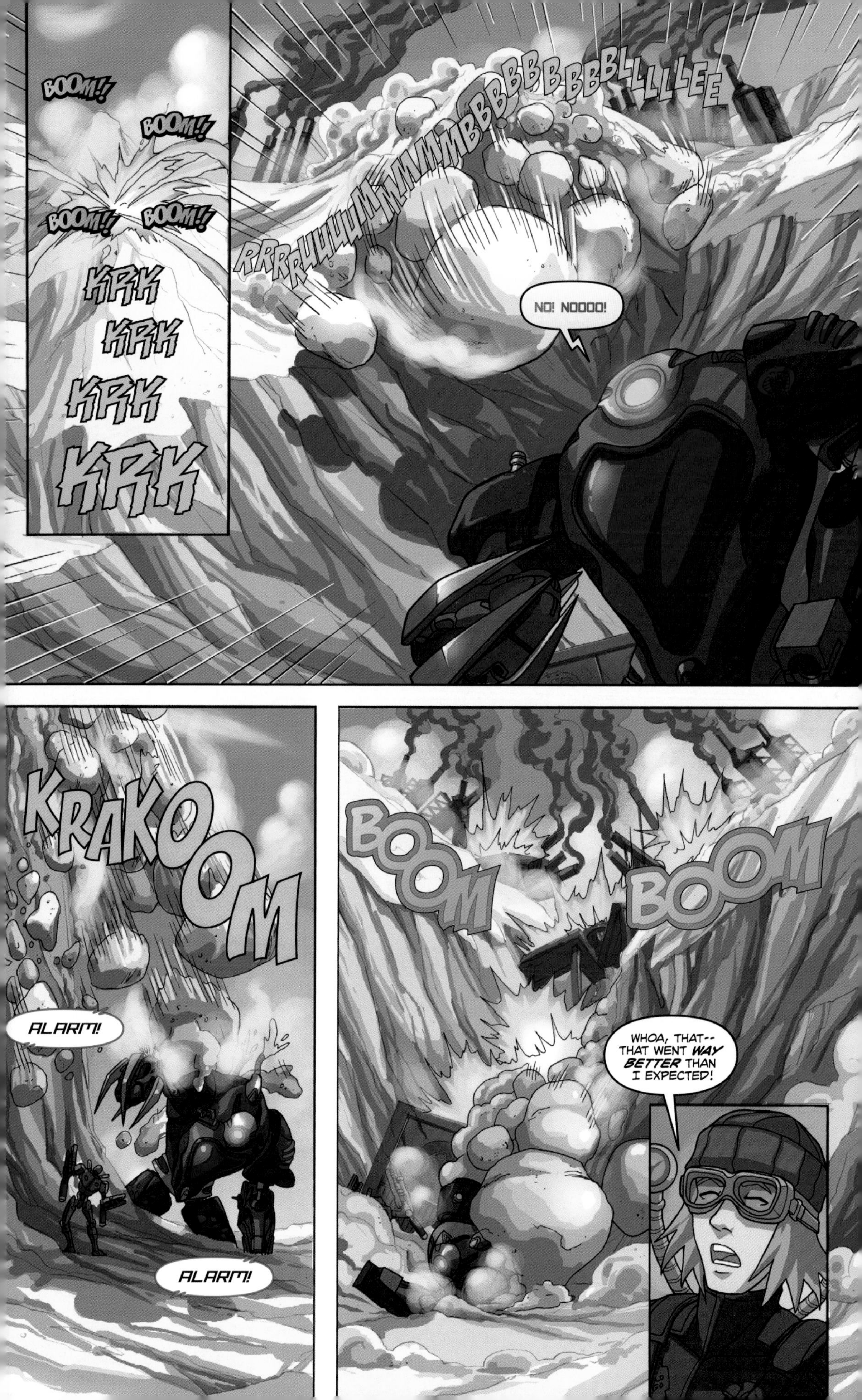
BOOM!!
BOOM!!
BOOM!!
BOOM!!
KRK
KRK
KRK
KRK
RRRRUUUUMMMMMMBBBBBBBLLLLLEE
NO! NOOOO!
KRAKOOOM
ALARM!
ALARM!
BOOOM
BOOOM
WHOA, THAT--
THAT WENT WAY BETTER THAN I EXPECTED!

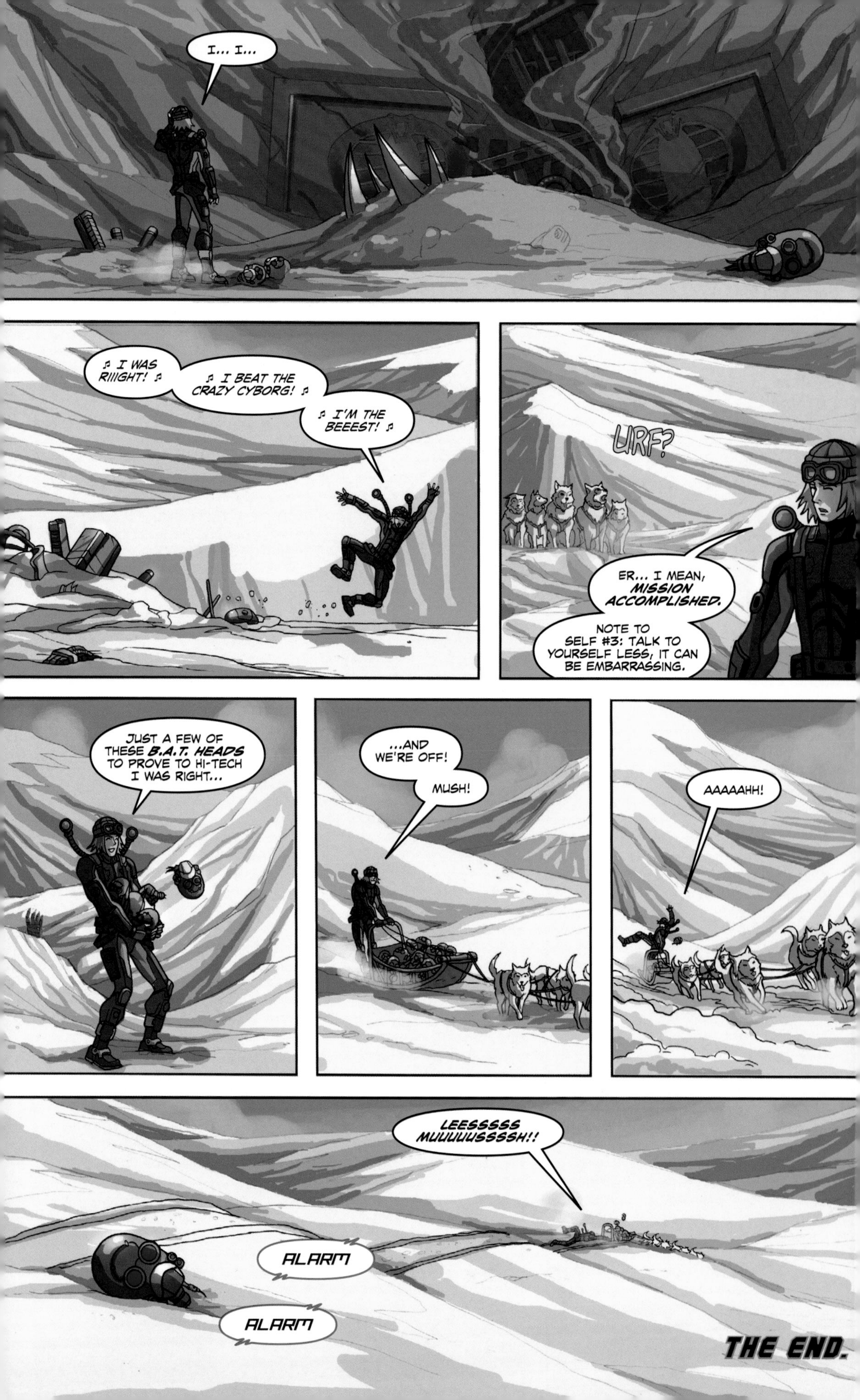
I... I...
♫ I WAS RIIIGHT! ♫
♫ I BEAT THE CRAZY CYBORG! ♫
♫ I'M THE BEEEST! ♫
URF?
ER... I MEAN, MISSION ACCOMPLISHED.
NOTE TO SELF #3: TALK TO YOURSELF LESS, IT CAN BE EMBARRASSING.
JUST A FEW OF THESE B.A.T. HEADS TO PROVE TO HI-TECH I WAS RIGHT...
...AND WE'RE OFF!
MUSH!
AAAAAHH!
LEESSSSS MUUUUUSSSSH!!
ALARM
ALARM
THE END.